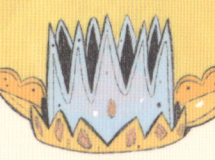

The Secret Fairy Club

ENCHANTED FOLK and *How to Find Them* IN THE WILD

Now you have proven yourself a loyal friend to fairies, it is time to reveal the other enchanted folk who live hidden in the human world.

To maintain the delicate balance of harmony between the magical and the human, we must do our very best to keep the sometimes-tricksy magical folk on our side. Contained within these precious pages are secrets that will both enlighten and aid us in that endeavour.

Guard this book with your life. Its truths must be protected at all costs.

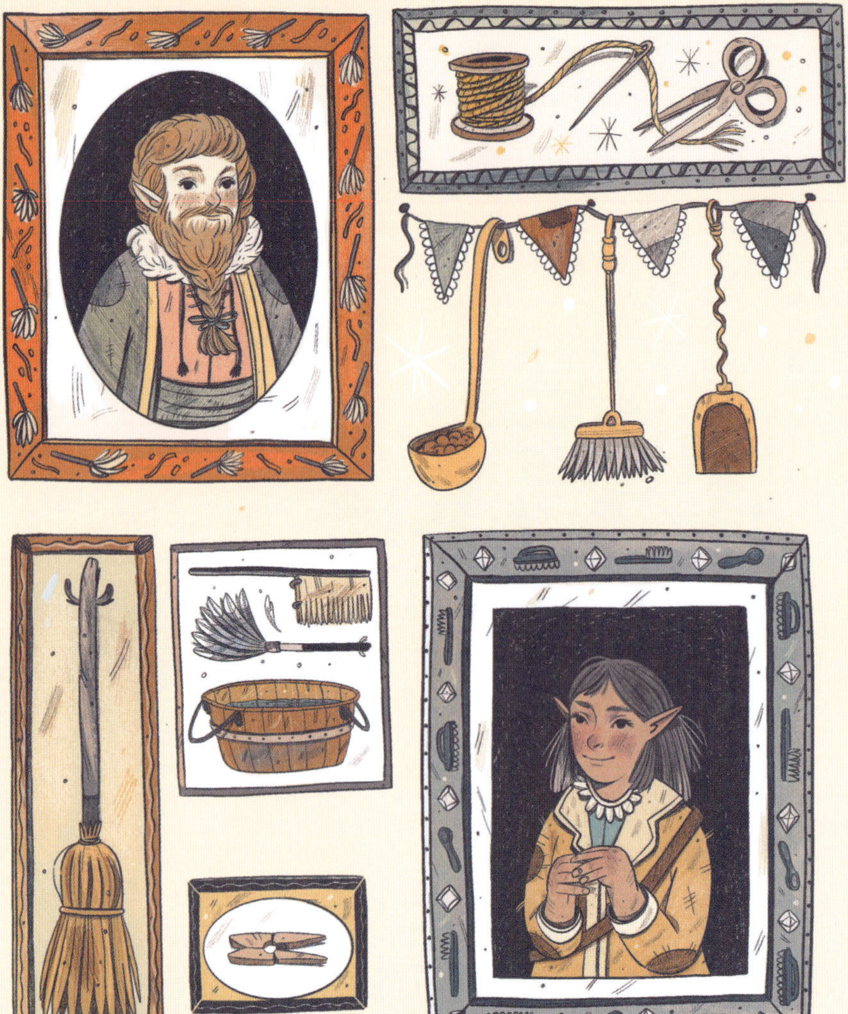

Hobgoblins and Brownies

Fairy folk can be found in every nook and cranny, and none more so than in the homes of humans.

Hobgoblins and brownies are diligent with their dusting! Young humans may marvel at how their mess seems to have magically tidied itself up of a morning. Their grown-ups may say different but, chances are, the resident hobgoblin or brownie has been busy in the night! But be warned… hobgoblins can show their ire by playing a prank on those who don't clean up their act!

While hobgoblins are mischievous, a brownie craves peace almost as much as it craves a laundry pile, and so it is rare for a hob and a brownie to live together, as the brownie will get very fed up with the hobgoblin's constant desire to play practical jokes.

Caring for Hobs and Brownies

Hobs or brownies may not want to be found... But they will always appreciate a tasty treat. Why not make some brownies for *your* brownie and leave them out at night?

A Warm Hearth

Hobgoblins and brownies are happiest when warm and cosy, but they stay out of sight of humans as much as possible.

A Hob's Top-Five Household Pranks

1) Unpairing socks and mixing them up – preferably in clashing colours.

2) Swapping the salt and the sugar.

3) Putting cling film over the toilet seat.

4) Telling the cat that the dog ate its dinner.

5) Spreading honey on the doorknobs.

Long, soft beards

A hob or brownie can dust even the most delicate of surfaces with their facial hair.

Tattered clothes

Never give a hob or brownie new clothes, unless you want them to flee and never come back! It is a badge of honour for them to wear raggedy clothes as it shows how proud they are of their hard work.

Enormous appetites

Despite their slight stature, a hob or brownie can guzzle more milk than a thirsty kitten and more porridge than Goldilocks and all three bears!

Finding Hobs and Brownies

As a sworn member of The Secret Fairy Club, these fellows *may* reveal themselves to you if they require your help. To encourage them to trust you, say these words three times, close your eyes and wrinkle your nose. If there's a hob in need in your home, they will appear before you as you open your eyes:

Hob, you help us.

Hob, we thank you.

Hob, may we now help you too?

Common Nesting Places

Drawers

Laundry basket

Sewing box

Dog basket

Fairy-Favoured and Famous!

Unlike his shyer brothers, there's one hobgoblin who shuns housework for fame and fairy favour. And he has the most important favour of all – that of King Oberon, husband to Queen Titania, and king of the fairies. The hob's name is Puck and, whatever you do, *never* let him trick you into joining his japes! It will always end well for Puck, but never for you...

Queen Titania, after Puck has given her a magic potion to make her fall in love with the next person she sees.

After Puck whispered in Mr William Shakespeare's ear as he dreamed one midsummer's night, the playwright gave the hob a starring role in one of his plays. Chaos ensued after Puck gave a love potion to Queen Titania that made her fall for a man whose head he'd just turned into that of a donkey...

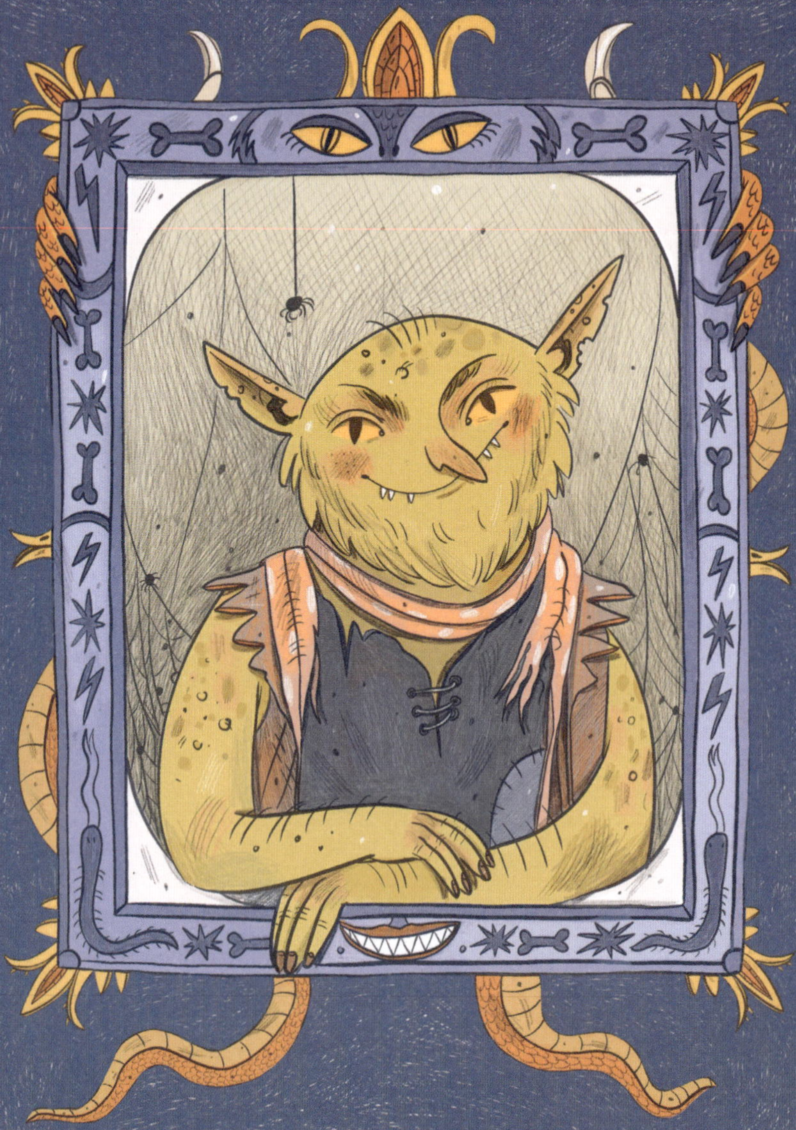

Goblins

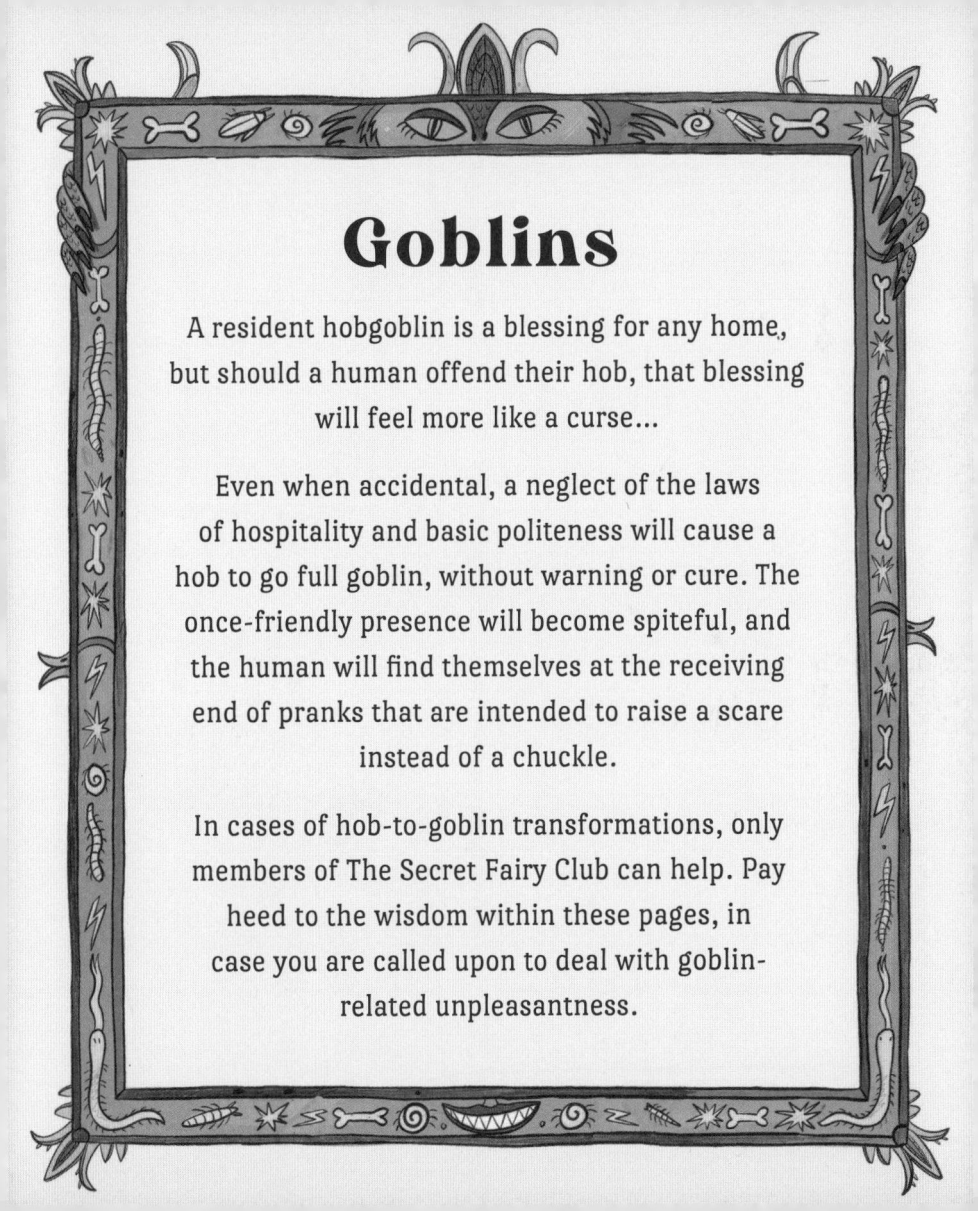

A resident hobgoblin is a blessing for any home, but should a human offend their hob, that blessing will feel more like a curse...

Even when accidental, a neglect of the laws of hospitality and basic politeness will cause a hob to go full goblin, without warning or cure. The once-friendly presence will become spiteful, and the human will find themselves at the receiving end of pranks that are intended to raise a scare instead of a chuckle.

In cases of hob-to-goblin transformations, only members of The Secret Fairy Club can help. Pay heed to the wisdom within these pages, in case you are called upon to deal with goblin-related unpleasantness.

Golden Rules for Goblin Avoidance

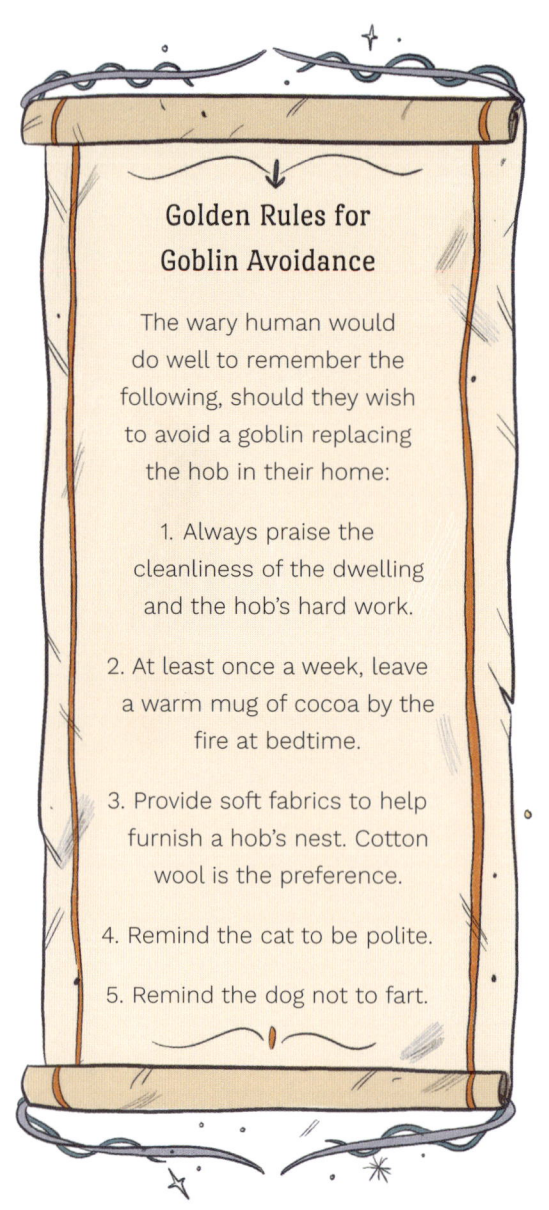

The wary human would do well to remember the following, should they wish to avoid a goblin replacing the hob in their home:

1. Always praise the cleanliness of the dwelling and the hob's hard work.

2. At least once a week, leave a warm mug of cocoa by the fire at bedtime.

3. Provide soft fabrics to help furnish a hob's nest. Cotton wool is the preference.

4. Remind the cat to be polite.

5. Remind the dog not to fart.

Gifts and Goodies

Goblins may be appeased with gifts, such as...

A pot of salve (for itchy goblin skin and painful boils)

A marshmallow (for tummies accustomed to dry bread and stagnant water)

A well-loved teddy bear (for something to cuddle that doesn't bite)

A joke book (for encouraging giggles, not grumbles)

If all else fails, this spell may be employed to turn a goblin back into a hob. Be wary, however – the incantation carries a high risk of leaving the spell-caster with goblin features of their own!

Hear me now, you goblin blight.

Deliver forth the peeve and spite.

Happy thoughts will set you free

to find the hob you used to be.

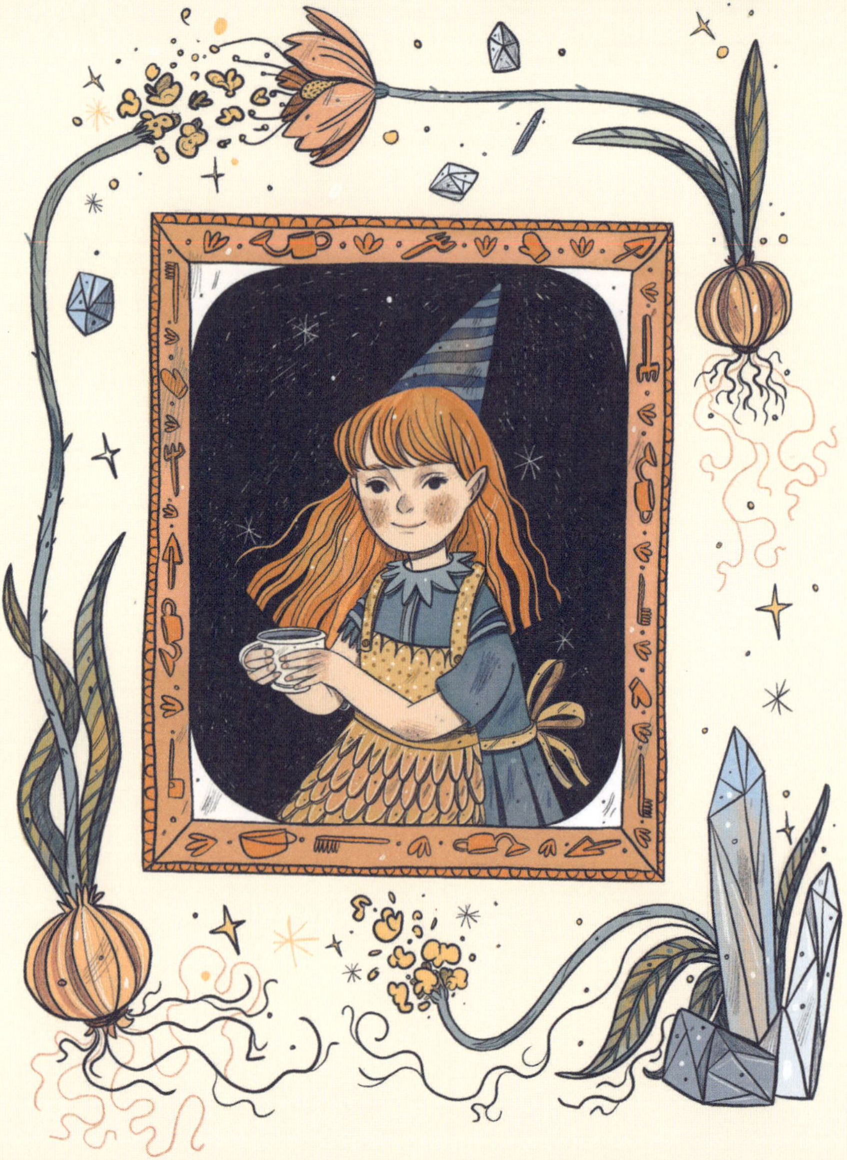

Gnomes

These shy, magical folk have a deep connection to the earth and its buried treasures. Some prefer to stay in their burrows deep underground and some live above the surface, like the jolly, colourful fellows that brighten up human gardens. As hobgoblins are to home and hearth, gnomes are dedicated to the world outside.

The gnomes that dwell above the ground only come alive once the sun goes down. They are able to turn themselves to stone in the daylight hours so humans don't realise that their garden ornaments are actually real magical creatures. The members of The Secret Fairy Club know better, and can help the gnomes by encouraging grown-ups to place them in areas of the garden, close to their burrowing holes... usually in darker corners, or wherever the soil is deepest and richest.

Guardians of Treasure

The gnomes are trusted protectors of all treasure that lies beneath the earth. Each gnome has its special responsibility.

Planting protectors

Guarding the bulbs and seeds that are planted for spring.

Dig protectors

Guarding the bones and fossils on archaeological digs.

Gem protectors
Guarding the precious gemstones and metals in mines.

The Pech

The mystery of the ancient monoliths that dot the Scottish landscape has baffled many a visitor. But magical folk and their allies have always known the truth – that every one of the ancient stones was heaved into place by a tribe of uncommonly strong gnomes known as The Pech. Like all gnomes, the Pech could not abide daylight, so did their building work in the depths of the night. The Secret Fairy Club has long protected the truth that when a Pech died, they were buried beneath a stone that they themselves had laid. Their spirit would return to the earth and imbue the stone with the gnome's fairy magic. There are no longer any living Pech in the world, but we can honour their work by visiting the stones and whispering our thanks for the beauty created by their toils.

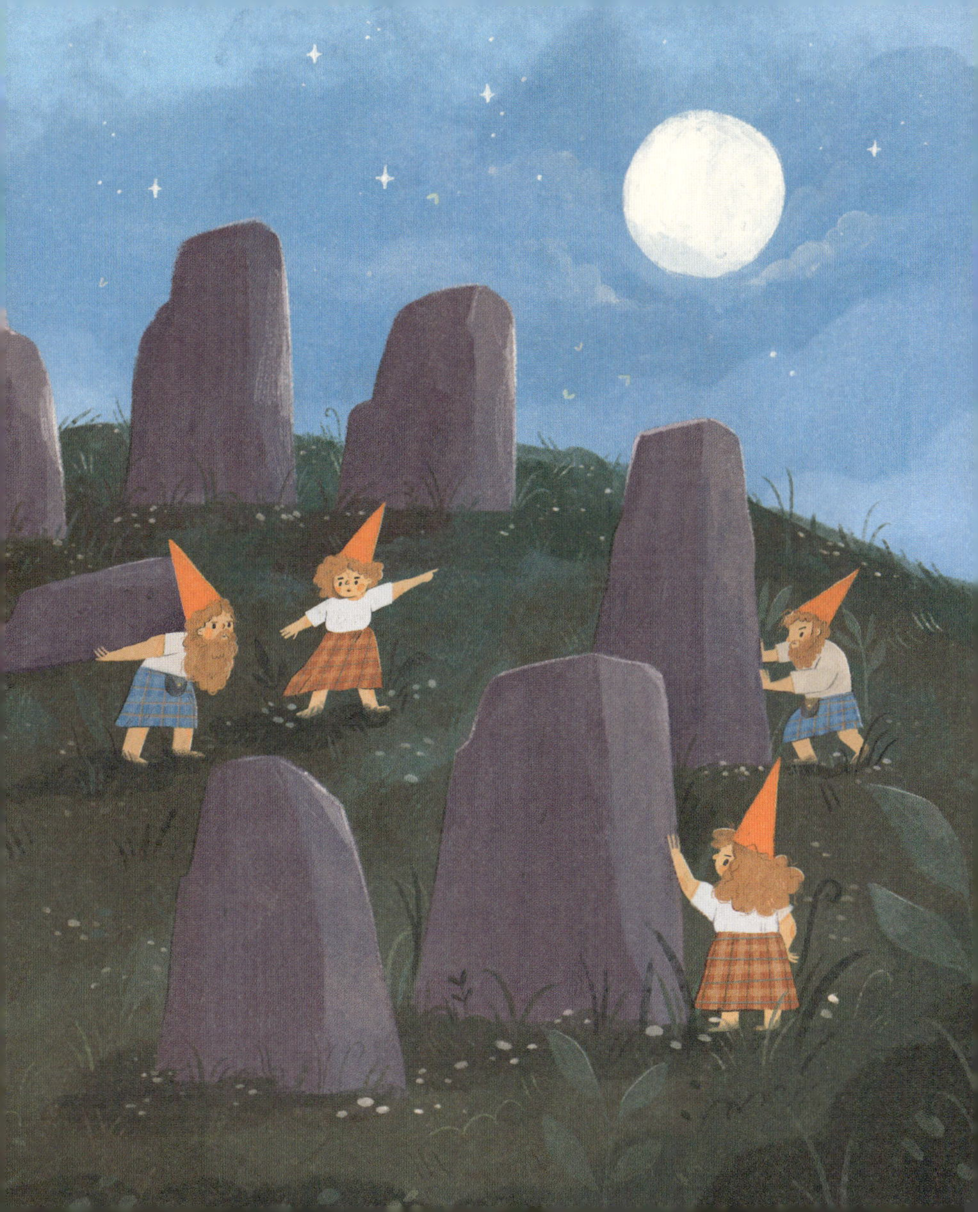

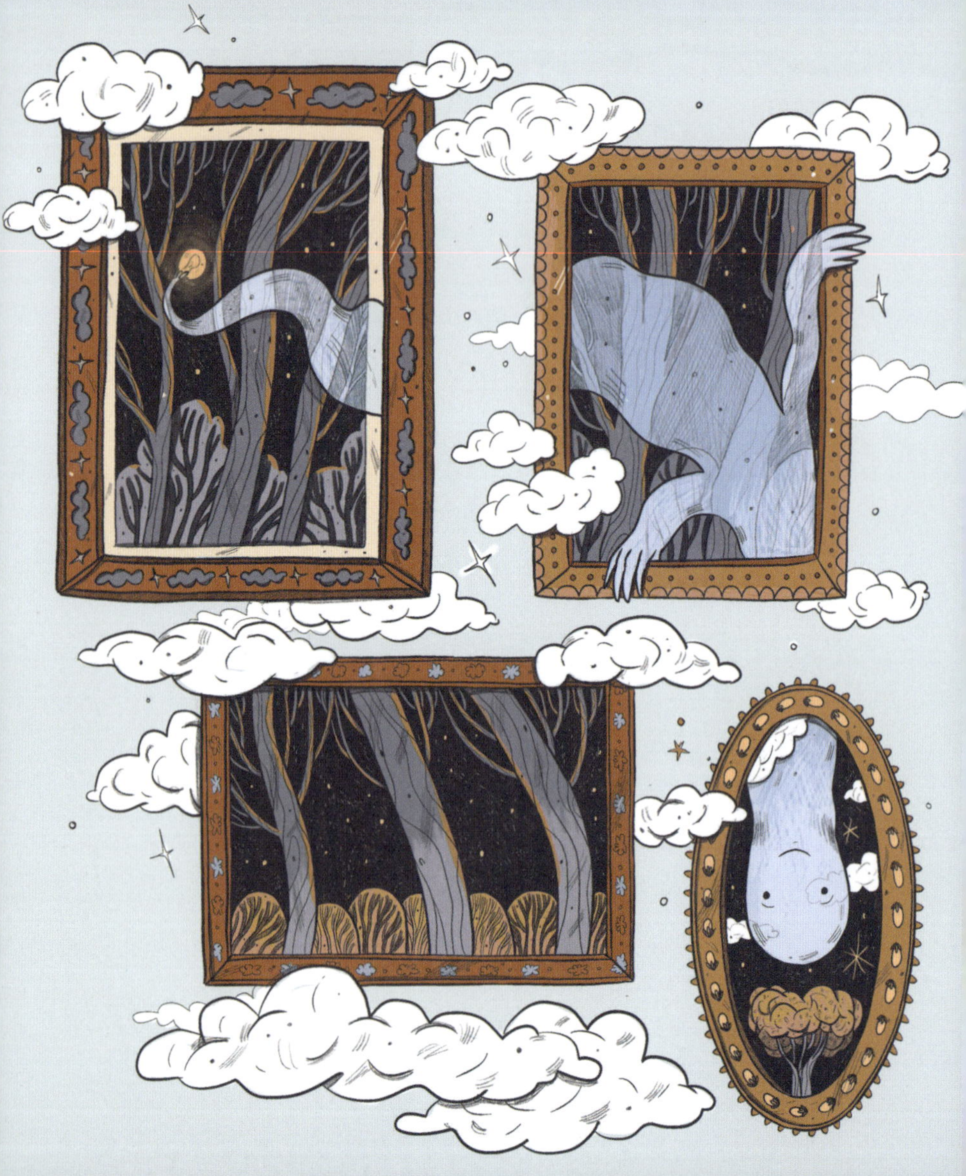

Sprites

The most difficult to find of the fairy folk, sprites are as insubstantial in body as the air around them.

Often mistaken for ghosts, sprites move by floating, wafting their way through their surroundings like a cloud. Sprites are sometimes mischievous, occasionally protective, and always unpredictable.

Night-time travellers on lonely roads must be especially cautious when it comes to sprites, as they take pleasure in leading humans from their chosen path. By following the sprite, who will be using their glow to entice and 'guide', a human will then find themselves lost and abandoned in the middle of nowhere as the sprite vanishes.

Will-o'-the-Wisp

Wispy by name and wispy by nature, this sprite prefers the environment of forests and woods. Humans who enjoy camping may well catch a glimpse of a will-o'-the-wisp, particularly if they need the loo in the middle of the night! Of course, The Secret Fairy Club would always advise 'holding it' until the morning if at all possible – for a will-o'-the-wisp will never miss a chance to lure a sleepy camper into the forest with its false light.

Headlamp

Wisps create their light by way of antennae with built-in lamps at their tips. These can be lit as bright as a stadium floodlight if the wisp chooses. They also have a choice of colours, just for fun.

Magical gas

Magic potions that are boiled turn to gas. When those potions contain flowers or other plant material, a will-o'-the-wisp is formed. While the body of a wisp cannot be called solid, it feels to the fingertips like the softest velvet and the smoothest silk, all at once.

Bioluminescence

Unlike other sprites, a wisp will never spontaneously combust into magical flames, however, it can create an attractive glow that radiates from its heart – and the fresher the air around it, the stronger their heart's glow will be.

> Should you find yourself lured by a wisp, remove your jacket, turn it inside out and put it back on again. It will break the enchantment and you can sternly remind the wisp not to mess with a Secret Fairy Club member.

Fairy Fire

Human travellers often report sightings of a phenomenon they call Fairy Fire, where rainbow flames seem to ignite out of thin air, often in boggy, swampy areas, and often at night. Scientists have offered a practical explanation, but The Secret Fairy Club and all fairy folk know the truth: it is the work of a sprite, indicating the location of buried treasure.

Charles Darwin, the renowned naturalist, reported a Fairy Fire while out at sea on his famous voyage aboard *HMS Beagle* in 1832. The Secret Fairy Club interviewed Mr Darwin upon his return, but is yet to find the treasure.

Being an ally to magical folk is a commitment that none should undertake lightly, for it must last a lifetime. Our grateful thanks go to you for taking the time to understand their foibles, delight in their differences and champion their needs. The more we can understand and educate ourselves, the better we can be in our protection and support of the magical beings that live around us.

Now, the biggest task of all lies ahead for you, Secret Fairy Club member and new friend of magical folk... You *must* keep the secrets revealed in this book locked deep within your heart and mind, only to be shared with others who have been inducted into this most secret of secret clubs.

You will know who to trust, if you trust your own heart to tell you so...

Cut out and keep your ten official Secret Fairy Club badges

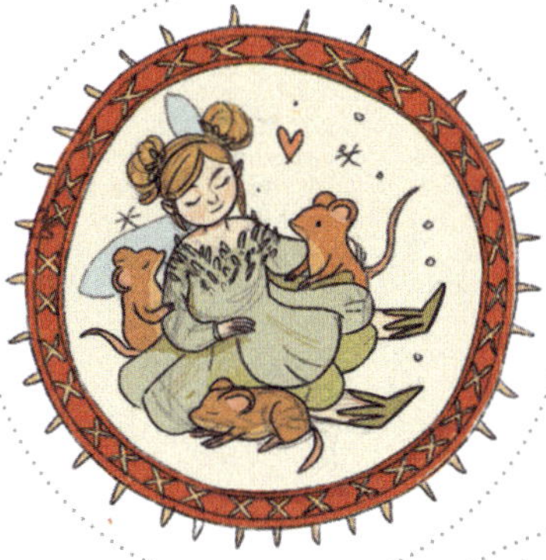

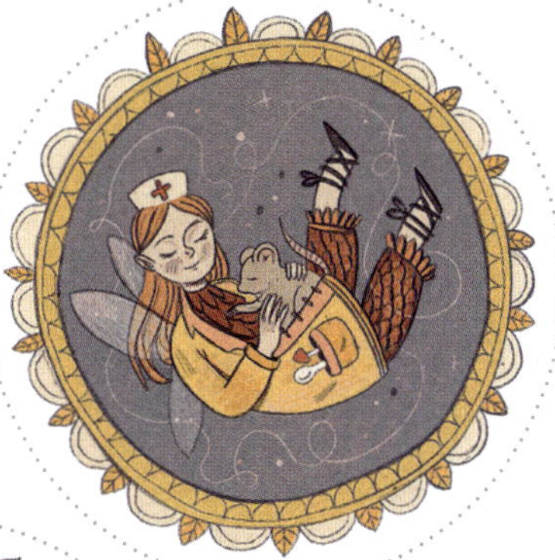

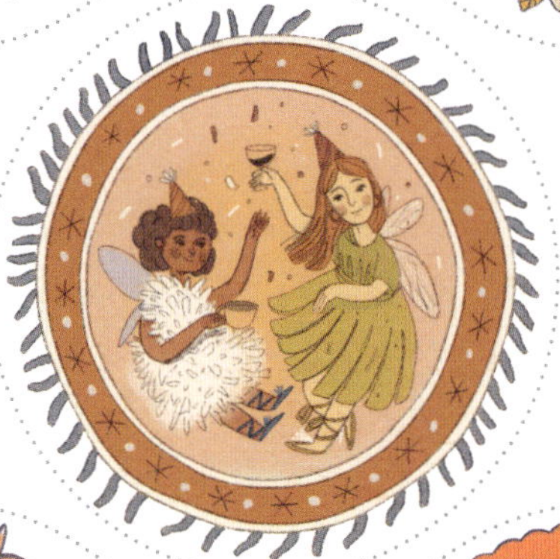

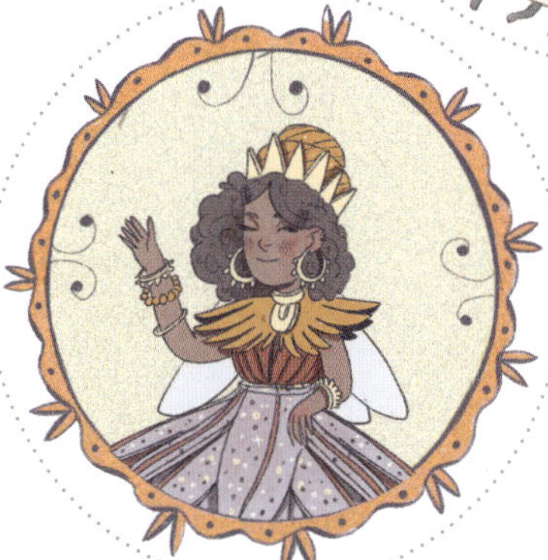

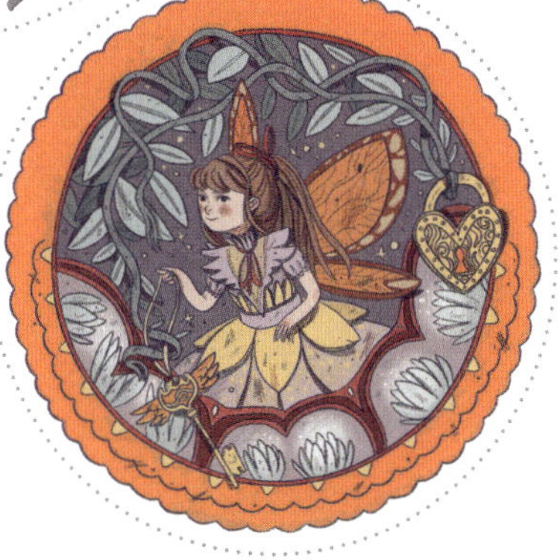